"Thank you mama, dry your eyes, there ain't no reason to cry
You made a genius and I, Ain't gonna take it for granted
I ain't gonna settle for lesser, I ain't gonna take what they handed
Nah, I'm gonna take what they owe me
And show you that I can fly"- Jermaine Cole

To my young kings and queens, I hope you are given permission to fly to heights that are unseen.

Your light is within, and I hope you have the village to remind you.

To my grandad for reminding me that I was capable of flying.

BLACK BOY FLY
BY: RAHEEM LOGAN
ILLUSTRATED BY: DELVONTE SMITH

Black

Rashad's smile shined brightest when the sun beamed in his eyes on hot summer days, as he watched the seagulls soar high in the bright blue sky.

He wanted to grow wings and fly with them, too. Each summer was full of weekend afternoons at the beach with his Mom and Pops.

Rashad would spend them playing in the sand, running through the water, and observing the seagulls above them.

Black Boy Fly 5

Watching them flap their strong wings against the wind floating in every direction gave Rashad a sense of calm.

For him, it was as if they were always flying in slow motion.

He was always in awe of despite how fast they were flying in the air, there seemed to be nothing that could shake the seagulls' peace of mind.

They never seemed to be out of control.

As they flew by and around him, Rashad never seemed to panic like everyone else.

He would close his eyes and smile, so he could hold on to the moments.

Rashad thought of how cool it would be to fly above the things that you were worried about or afraid of on the ground.

The beach was a long drive from Harlem, so they only went during the summer. He was always excited when summertime came around.

His black melanin glowed in the sun and his bare feet felt free digging into the sand with every step; there were no worries at the beach.

It was a second home because of how special it made him feel.

The fresh breeze rubbing against his face, running on the sand, the gulls, and his whole family being together in one place brought him a happiness that he never wanted to let go of.

Then the arguments started, then he would see them together less.

Rashad's parents' split was complete just after his ninth birthday, and the beach trips were becoming a distant memory.

He hadn't gone in two summers.

He could not fully understand what was happening around him, but he really wanted to go back to the beach.

First he got some maybe's, then he stopped getting responses to the question.

He stopped asking after a few times.

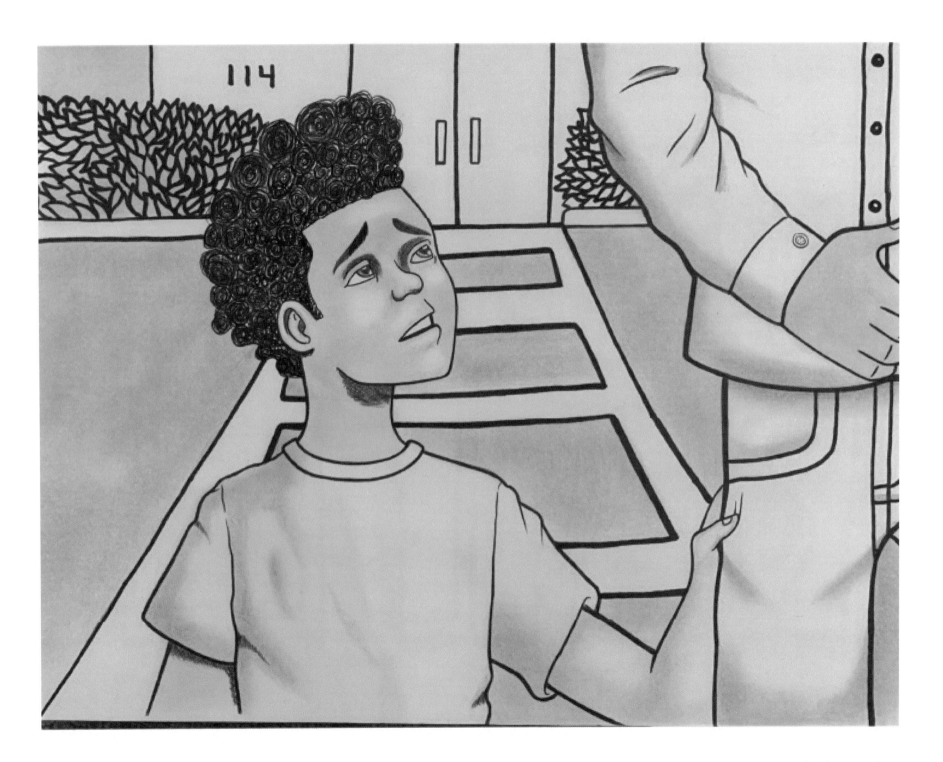

Black Boy Fly 9

Everything was being split up. He had to keep some clothes and toys at his father's crib. He was not having it.

There was one thing they decided not to cancel.

Rashad's mom put a down payment on squash lessons and both of them were paying for it. She trusted her co-worker, but never heard of the sport.

Squash? The vegetable? Yes squash is a vegetable, but nahhh.
Squash was like Tennis and Racquetball, but not exactly one or the other.
Rashad played neither.
He remembered what his mom said about trying things before you judge them. He also remembered the adults he watched judge things every day.

There were courts on the part of the city next to the buildings where the rich people lived. It wasn't too far from home, but it felt like a different world in just a few blocks.
It was his first organized sport.

As Rashad, for the first time, approached the doors to enter the Upper West Squash Club, he was excited and nervous.

"Squash is Whaack," Rashad remembered the voices of his friends when he told them about squash. His friends clowned him for it. What was unfamiliar was assumed to be whack; there was nothing to argue.

He couldn't believe how close it was to home and how many times he had walked pass the place before. It was hard to miss, but he had no reason to pay attention to it before.

When the doorman walked with them to the elevator, Rashad noticed something: This was also the only reason his parents spent more than ten minutes together in a long time.

When his parents dropped him off for his first day, they both were in such a rush to leave.

They signed the papers they needed to, told him to be careful, behave, and said one of them would return in a couple of hours.

They both had left work and had to get back to it.

They missed or just didn't mention that besides the ball, Rashad was the only black person or object in the space.

He looked around and saw that there was no one that looked like him around.

Until this point in his life, he had never been the only one with dark skin in any place.

Basically everyone was in a suit and looked too serious. It felt like a big library. From the shiny floors in the lobby to the dust free red carpets on each foor, Rashad had only seen things like this on TV.

He wasn't sure if he belonged there.

One of the coaches introduced himself to Rashad and handed him a racquet.

The racquet was red, and the strings were black.

The racquet felt light as a feather and he was told that he would be able to hit the ball as hard as he could against the wall.

Rashad was trying to decide if the racquet was a sword or that thing Ma uses to get the flies.

The coach led him to the court to tell him first about safety and hitting the ball.

His eyes lit up like it was mom's home cooking waiting for him.

He really wanted to try, so he did. He ran to the middle of the squash court, threw the ball in the air, and with perfect timing smacked the ball to the front of the court.

The ball sprung out off the racquet like a slingshot and bounced back against the wall.
BOOM!! At least that is what it sounded like to Rashad given how quiet it was.

The ball then flew back just over Rashad's head to the back glass that was behind them.

They looked at each other in silence.

Rashad didn't know if he was in trouble or if he did something right. He turned around slowly. He knew from school how adults treated kids that did not follow the rules.

He also didn't know the rules to squash and wasn't sure if what he did was right or wrong.

He hit the ball though, right? At least he didn't miss.
There was something else though.

Something about the sound when the ball traveled to the wall and bounced off it, Rashad saw calm in.

For how quickly that ball had floated by and over him, there was something else that caught Rashad's attention.

It moved like it was always in control. How? Rashad wondered.

He was not sure, but he was going to explore and find out.

The coach's eyes lit up because he wasn't sure if Rashad got lucky or if he was a star in the making.

With a real serious face then a smile he said, " You have the wrong shoes on. Good shot though."

Realizing he did something right on the shot, he yelled, "Yurrrrrr," out of pure excitement for what was ahead.

The young members were not as excited about Rashad's arrival.

The kids were mostly older than him, and they all looked different than him.
His shoes were fresh out the box.
Theirs were worn out but wearable.
His hair was medium length and a little nappy. Theirs was a little shorter, more conditioned and straightened.

His skin was chocolate brown, and theirs went between beige, vanilla or a lightly toasted marshmallow.

A few of the players treated Rashad like a regular kid, asking how long he had been playing and what video games he liked.

Some looked right through him, others looked at him like an animal at the zoo.

A few would stare and talk about him, but never walk up to him.

A few city blocks separated these kids, and while they've seen people that looked different from them before, most of them never had to interact with them.

Rashad had to prove himself in the first week.

After practice one day, one of the kids tried to make fun of Rashad by asking him, "Why are you so black?"
"OOOOOOOOOOHHHHHHH!"- An instigator followed.

The other kids started yelling and surrounded them both. They hoped a fight would happen.
Rashad wanted no part of one.

It was his first week, and the kid weighed like twenty pounds more than him, so it probably wasn't the smartest choice.

Rashad had never been asked this question before, but he also was not someone who panicked under pressure.

He knew he had to stand up for himself though because nothing would be the same if he didn't.

Rashad looked around at all the eyes on him and remembered a joke that his friend told him that would help in this situation.

"Who here likes chocolate milk better than regular milk?" he yelled out.

All the kids looked at one another and raised their hands as they awkwardly laughed at the same time.

 "Looks like I have the skin color that all of you like, so it looks like you are asking the wrong question."

They all stood in silence.

Then one kid said, "Well, he's got a point,"

Another said, "Is that why my parents go to the beach all the time? Because they do come back home darker than they were before."

Without a single punch thrown, Rashad confidently walked out of the locker room.

Boy

That didn't mean that the altercation didn't effect him.

He never told his parents about what happened.

Partly because he did not know how to, but also because they wouldn't listen.

If they wasn't hearing him about the beach, why would they listen now?

Rashad wanted to understand the calm that the ball floated around with.

He kept hitting the little rubber ball again and again to make sure he was learning as much as he could.

Squash tested his body, and it also made him think a lot.

He liked how quickly he had to think of solutions and adjust to how the ball was moving around him.

Before Rashad would hit the ball, he slowed down just like he imagined watching the seagulls approaching him.

He then would focus and kick out his right leg like he saw Serena and Venus do in tennis to hit a backhand, his favorite shot.

As the strings of Rashad's racquet struck the ball, it would explode off those strings like the sound of a shooting cannon, but with the speed of a bullet.

He would practice this same motion time and time again because of the feeling it gave him.

Rashad earned the opportunity to begin competing in tournaments quickly.

Rashad felt that competition brought out the worst in a lot of people, and Rashad was nervous because he was afraid it would do the same to him.

He always focused on having fun and not about whether he won or lost.

He tried his hardest in everything he did. He chased every shot down as if it were the last point. He competed like he constantly had something to prove. Not to others, but to himself.

While he was focused on having fun, Rashad would look behind him every time other people were watching.

It was as if he was looking for something or someone that he could never find.

But he always managed to keep his cool.

What separated him from his peers was his sportsmanship.

Even when he lost, Rashad always hugged his opponents and congratulated them.

Most of his opponents were confused when he did it, but he was just excited to be playing.

There was something deeper with the sport as well.

Being able to play squash and run around as much as he did reminded Rashad of his happy place: The beach.

The wood and sand surfaces were different, but the feelings were the same.

However, as happy as it made him, there was still something missing.

Rashad squashed through a lot of competition, and in two years he became one of the best at the club.

Nobody had heard of a kid from Harlem playing squash, let alone being good at it.

He made sure to remind people where he was from.

Even though they weren't together anymore, his momma and dad were both working to pay for him to play. He wanted to make them proud.

Squash felt like the last thing on either one of their minds.

They never seemed to be interested in talking about it with him.
It felt like they were either too busy with their lives or their phones to pay Rashad any mind.

"That's good," and "Good," was the furthest he got with their responses when he talked about squash.

He remembered asking each of his parents if they could watch him play sometime.

They always said either "Next time," or did not respond at all.

Their silence told Rashad all that he needed to know.

After a while, just like him asking to go back to the beach, he learned to stop asking.

Pops was Mr. Fix-It for the whole St. Nicholas Terrace block that Rashad grew up on.

He was very good with his hands, and always knew how to solve most problems in an apartment.

He was very respected for how willing he was to help other people.

Moms was a social worker for the state of New York.

She did not speak often, but when she spoke, everyone made sure they paid attention.

Her words made those around her feel just a little bit better about their situation. She had that kind of spirit.

They spent so much of their lives fixing other people's problems that they lost sight of a problem growing right in front of them.

Nearly two years had gone by, and neither one showed up to watch Rashad play.

However, they were never late to pick him up once he was done. One of them always showed up in front of the squash club to pick him up on time. Neither his Mom nor Dad wanted to look like THAT parent by showing up late.

They always made a point that one of them would get it done.

Rashad was now Eleven years old; his club hosted the U.S. Junior Championships tournament. Hundreds of kids from around the country arrived in New York City to compete.

He was still the only black person in the space.

It was the first time he had the chance to compete in this tournament, and he wanted to see how he would do.

After a pre-tournament practice with a few of the kids from his club, Rashad was stretching, when a parent that had been watching him play introduced herself and began talking to him.

She said, "You're really good at this sport. Your parents must be so proud to watch you play.

Are they coming to watch this weekend?"

Rashad's first thought was, "Why is this lady asking me about my parents?" It was the first time someone in that space asked him about them coming.

He stopped asking them and tried forgetting. He tried really hard.

It was the one thing he really wanted but he had no control of: his family being together.

He dared not ever get his hopes up. The thought never went away though.

A stranger pressed the one button that left Rashad without a response.
He didn't know what to do.

Realizing that he never answered the woman's question, Rashad's heart started to pump faster than it ever pumped before.

His eyes started to fill as quickly as the open fire hydrants pushing out water on the hot summer days.

He looked at this woman, then around the area at all the other players. Everyone was with their parents or someone, except Rashad.

In a space of over 150 people, Rashad couldn't have felt more alone.

He felt one drop coming down his left cheek, then his right. He tried to wipe them away, but they kept coming.

Rashad felt weak because no one talked to him about what to do when the tears start to fall. Not unless you fell or something. He remembered making fun of those kids crying with no scars or bruises to show. He didn't know.

Maybe their hearts were hurting, just like his was at that moment.

He quickly ran pass the woman into the locker room to change, and then snuck to the nearest staircase and dashed down the stairs, then out of the club onto the streets and sun of the spring.

<u>Fly</u>

Rashad weaved around and in-between the older people crowding the streets. The adults reminded him of his parents because they just scrolled through their phones like he wasn't there.

An 11 year old running through the streets by themselves might spark some attention. Everyone one else assumed another person would do something about it.

Rashad made it back to his block. As he was approaching his building, brother Tommy was standing by the steps leading up to the entrance.

Rashad had seen Tommy before, but only his parents had ever really talked to him. Rashad remembered him because he always had a suit on like he was going somewhere important.

Tommy was also one of the few people that he saw that looked cool with glasses on. Rashad couldn't tell his age, but he had some grey hair on his face, so he was just old.

He respected his elders and knew from experience, old people don't like to tell other people their age.

Black Boy Fly 47

Tommy was known as one of the smartest people on the block, and he chose his words wisely.

He kept his sentences short, but he was never misunderstood.

People thought that Tommy had no job. Tommy had one, but no one ever asked what it was.

He was always on the steps of the apartment building entrance, whenever Rashad left for school and when he returned home.

Tommy always happened to be in the right place at the right time. Outside of that, he just observed the streets before him.

With Rashad still wiping away the tears on the steps, he looked over at Tommy.

"Aren't you going to ask me what's wrong? Rashad said.

"I didn't and yet, here we are." Tommy responded. "What's going on though? You're here earlier than normal."

"It's my moms and pops," Rashad started. Tommy quickly cut him off.

"They're not here, I can see that. Either you ran off from wherever you were supposed to be, or you ran off from wherever you were supposed to be. Your mom and pops are going to come looking for you."

"They don't care."

"Dont care about what? They gave you life, slick"- brother Tommy responded as he cut him off again.

"They don't care about me playing squash. Moms signed me up, but she never watched me play in two years. Neither of them have."

Tommy thought about saying something, then he realized that he needed to listen.

I like playing it a lot, but it has never felt important enough for them to pay attention. And it is so lonely out there sometimes..."

As he spoke, the tears started to come back into his eyes and his voice started to crack.

"...Looking different than everyone. I always look back when I play hoping they would surprise me, but they're never there. One or both of them always says next time. Still hasn't happened."

Black Boy Fly 51

It was the first time that he said it aloud to anyone.

Rashad looked up at Tommy wanting a response and felt like a weight was lifted finally speaking those words to another person.

Tommy looked at him and placed his right hand on his chin hair, thinking. Three words came out: "Gotta tell them."
"Tell them what?"
"Exactly what you just told me."
"Why do I have to tell them? They're my parents. Shouldn't THEY know these things?"

"If you just told me all that, then you can tell them the same thing, Rashad," Tommy told him.

"Not saying they're right in anyway. But they're not mind readers, they're people. Even adults do not have it all figured out."

As Tommy spotted Rashad's mom and dad coming up the block, he said to him, "Good luck kid, moms and pops coming in 5,4,3,2,1." As Rashad's eyes switched to his parents rushing up the hill then back at Tommy, he was gone.

He never learned what Tommy did for a living.

"Get Upstairs. Now," his mom said, without moving her teeth.

When the three of them entered his mom's apartment, "RASHAD ERMIAS BROWN, sit down," His mom said with the really serious voice.

She never raised her voice, but once her voice got like that and she said his full name, he knew what it meant: He better start talking.

"First Off, Where were you going, though, really? You had enough for a one way bus fare and no snacks.

Second of all, You lucky the cops didn't get involved. Nobody wants or needs any of that around here.

And third, How no one saw you leave without an adult is what I'm trying to figure out."
She was heated.

Rashad sat in the center of the couch and his parents pulled up two chairs and looked at him, waiting for him to say something.

He knew whether or not he spoke up, further punishment was coming. He had nothing to lose, really.

So he took a deep breath and started speaking... Just as he did with Tommy, telling his parents his truth. He felt like they didn't care. He felt lonely at competitions being different from everyone and them never being there to support him.

With each word, they looked at each other, looked at the tears in their child's eyes and silently their eyes filled with them, too.

It was the first time that either one of them cried in front of their child.

"It just would mean everything if you both came to watch me," Rashad finished.

Rashad's mom and dad looked at each other without saying a word, and understood. Support was not coming in the form of quality time with their son.

They both got out of their chairs and joined him on the couch.

"We're so sorry, Ra", they said together, in disappointment with themselves. "We're so sorry that we put work and ourselves before you for so long. We love you so much. We messed up, and we're gonna do better with balance, we promise. Can you forgive us?"

Forgive? Did he hear the words sorry twice? Whenever sorry was said, HE was always apologizing for something. He couldn't help but smile a little bit.

He did not believe what he was hearing. He pinched his arm to make sure this was real.
His parents were telling him that they were wrong.

Rashad knew he had his parents in a good spot, and he didn't want to take this rare opportunity for granted.

"Well, there's this tournament that I'm playing in this weekend, actually, for the top spot in the country in my age group."
"Wait, I saw an email about this a couple weeks ago, but I glanced passed it," his dad said.
"This is why I should be getting these emails," Mom said smiling rolling her eyes.

They all laughed. It was a long time since they all did that together.

They both went to separate rooms with their phones. Two quick phones calls were made. They both canceled any other weekend plans.

The next morning, as Rashad was walking out with his Momma to meet his Pops at the subway, he spotted Tommy. In the same suit, same spot, just watching the streets over him.

Rashad was going to say something to Tommy when their eyes met, but he didn't have to. Tommy nodded showing respect to the brave young boy that took his advice.

Rashad arrived about 30 minutes before his start time for his first round match. It was the first time they showed up early. It was the first time since his first day that they had been upstairs together. His moms and pops were just as amazed by the club as Rashad had been two years ago.

As Rashad was finishing checking in, His dad said, "Good luck, Ra. Have fun and you know what to do. Oh, yeah, I forgot to tell you, real men cry. I'm sorry we're just having this conversation, but please don't you forget that. You are strong for what you did. I love you." He kissed him on his forehead.

"You know you're on punishment after this tournament is over. Don't think we forgot about you running away," his mom said, smiling and kissing his cheek.
He had hoped she was joking, but he wasn't sure.
He pretended not to hear that part.

"Ra, I know you've been special since the day I first held you in my arms, and I hope you show everyone here that. Please don't ever forget who you are. I'll always be with you in case you do. Show them that Harlem is here to represent."

The tournament officials called for him. It was time.

As Rashad's mom looked in her son's beautiful brown eyes, she smiled and said one more thing that she had never said to him before:

"Fly, black boy, fly."

As Rashad walked towards the court, he closed his eyes and smiled, just as he did when he used to go to the beach.

He imagined his wings growing and rising above the pain that he had felt in the same place a day before.

Rashad felt as powerful as the birds he admired.

If only for this moment, Rashad's parents were together, for him, finally watching him doing what he loved. Whether he won or lost didn't matter to him.

In his mind, he had nothing to worry about.

Black Boy Fly 63

About the Author:

Raheem Logan is a compassionate leader, educator, and community builder focused on empowering un- derrepresented youth in predominately white spaces. He has created culturally conscious teachings to bring honest, reflective, and transparent dialogue in the classroom and as a coach on the squash court.

Born and raised in Harlem, NY, Raheem comes with over fifteen years experience playing and coaching squash. He was elected captain of his team, earned two all conference selections and received his BA from Wesleyan University in Sociology. He has served as a leader and panelist on the Laureus Sport For Good New York Initiative and We Coach, both focusing on Sports Based Youth Development. Black Boy Fly is his first book.

CPSIA information can be obtained at www.ICGtesting.com
Printed in the USA
LVIW012354111120
671366LV00016B/230

9 781735 632506